MO'S MISCHIEF

Teacher's Pet

Other titles in the Mo's Mischief series:

Four Troublemakers
Teacher's Pet
Pesky Monkeys
You're No Fun, Mum!

MO'S MISCHIEF

Teacher's Pet

Hongying Yang

HarperCollins *Children's Books*

First published in China by Jieli Publishing House 2003
First published in Great Britain by HarperCollins *Children's Books* 2008
HarperCollins *Children's Books* is a division of HarperCollins*Publishers* Ltd
77-85 Fulham Palace Road, Hammersmith, London W6 8JB

The HarperCollins *Children's Books* website address is
www.harpercollinschildrensbooks.co.uk

1

Text copyright © Hongying Yang 2003
English translation © HarperCollins Publishers 2008

Illustrations © Pencil Tip Culture & Art Co 2003

Hongying Yang asserts the moral right to be identified
as the author of this work

ISBN-13 978-0-00-727340-9
ISBN-10 0-00-727340-1

Printed and bound in England by
Clays Ltd, St Ives plc

Mixed Sources
Product group from well-managed
forests and other controlled sources
www.fsc.org Cert no. SW-COC-1806
© 1996 Forest Stewardship Council

FSC is a non-profit international organisation established to promote the
responsible management of the world's forests. Products carrying the FSC
label are independently certified to assure consumers that they come
from forests that are managed to meet the social, economic and
ecological needs of present and future generations.

Find out more about HarperCollins and the environment at
www.harpercollins.co.uk/green

TEACHER'S PET

Mo and Man-Man had always been in the same class, ever since they'd started school together at three years old. Even in nursery class, Man-Man had been the teacher's pet. She was always well behaved and boring.

Mo, on the other hand, was always naughty and full of mischief. He and Man-Man could not have been more different.

When they started primary school, the teacher asked Man-Man to keep a special eye on Mo to make sure he didn't get up to anything.

Man-Man took this job very seriously; she kept an eye on Mo all day long. She did not let Mo out of her sight... except, of course, when Mo went to the toilet. Man-Man thought going into the boys' toilets was beyond the call of duty.

The strange thing was that Mo didn't mind Man-Man watching him all the time. In fact, he liked it. He worshipped Man-Man. He couldn't remember the names of any other girls from school, but he was always talking about Man-Man when he got home.

"Hey Mum, Man-Man got another star today for being good. She's got more stars then anyone else in the class."

"Hey, Mum, Man-Man ate every little bit of her dinner today, and even cleared her plate away."

"Hey, Mum, Man-Man painted a lovely picture today. The teacher put it up on the wall."

But that was way back when Mo was very young. Now that he was older, he didn't like Man-Man at all.

The fact that Mo once worshipped Man-Man was a secret he had never told anybody, not even his best friends Da, Mao and Fei – better known as Hippo, Monkey and Penguin. If they

found out he had ever liked Man-Man they would laugh their heads off.

Mo couldn't quite remember when he stopped liking Man-Man, but he could certainly remember why.

It was in Year Two. At the end of playtime, the children had to line up in two lines: boys in one, and girls in the other. They had to hold each other's hands as they walked back into school. After playtime on their first day in Year Two, Penguin was standing next to Lingau, so he took *her* hand. Hippo was next to Angel, so he took *her* hand. Monkey was next to Joy, so he took *her* hand. Mo was standing next to Man-Man so he held her hand very firmly. But Man-Man pushed his hand out of the way, and went over and held Wen's hand instead!

Wen Tao Ting was a goody-two-shoes sort of boy who always combed his hair back neatly and acted politely.

Mo hated him.

Although Wen was the same age as Mo, he had already learned to read more than 1000 Chinese characters. Wen could do multiplication and division and he could recite poetry from memory. Worse, not only did the teachers admire Wen, *girls* admired Wen too.

It didn't bother Mo that Man-Man didn't want to hold his hand. But it *did* bother him that she wanted to hold Wen's instead! He decided to tell their class teacher.

"Ms Qin, Man-Man won't let me hold her hand."

"He grabbed my hand too tight and it hurt!" Man-Man said, quickly.

Ms Qin said Mo was bullying Man-Man and told him to stop.

It wasn't fair. Mo said he hadn't hurt Man-Man on purpose. But no matter how much he explained, Ms Qin didn't believe him. Ms Qin only believed what Man-Man said, because Man-Man was so well behaved, whereas Mo was always up to something.

And *that* was why Mo had stopped liking Man-Man.

By the time Mo was in Year Three, he had become *really* mischievous! Now, Ms Qin couldn't possibly keep an eye on Mo every minute of the day and in every class. Ms Qin needed someone to keep an eye on Mo, and that someone had to be responsible and fair. Who better than Man-Man, the teacher's pet?!

Ms Qin sidled up at Man-Man at the end of school one day. "I'm going to ask you to sit next to Mo, because I want you to keep him out of mischief. What do you think, Man-Man? Will you do it?"

"Yes, Ms Qin, I'll do it."

But Man-Man didn't *really* want to sit next to Mo. She really wanted to sit next to Wen. Wen and Mo were so different, it was as if they came from two different planets. Mo was noisy and mischievous. He loved to play practical jokes on people. Wen was studious and liked to read books. Wen had read so many books, there wasn't a thing he didn't know. He nickname was Little Encyclopedia because he knew so much! Man-Man had always wanted to sit next Wen.

But Ms Qin had asked her to sit next to Mo. And

Man-Man was so well behaved that it would never occur to her to say no!

Ms Qin gave Man-Man a notebook and asked her to write down all of Mo's mischievous acts – she called them "Mo's Mischief". Man-Man had to give the notebook to Ms Qin at the end of school each day, so that Ms Qin knew exactly what Mo had been up to.

On the first day of the new seating arrangement, Mo smiled at Man-Man... but she didn't smile back.

Mo tried to start a conversation with his new deskmate. "Man-Man, why are you looking so serious? We used to be friends in nursery!"

Man-Man didn't bother to reply. She just wrote and wrote in that little notebook...

Mo didn't like the way Man-Man was acting. Could this really be the Man-Man he had liked so much when he was younger?

When Mo found out that Man-Man had been asked by Ms Qin to keep an eye on him, he decided to teach her a lesson.

It was when they were doing Maths. Man-Man put up her hand to answer a question. Then she stood up so that the whole class could hear her answer. Mo had an idea. He carefully moved Man-Man's chair a little bit. He did this with his feet, while pretending to be sitting perfectly upright. He acted as if he was paying close attention to Man-Man's answer, nodding his head from time to time to show how carefully he was listening.

"Very good, Man-Man. An *excellent* answer," said the teacher. "You may sit down."

There was a loud *thump* as Man-Man's bum hit the floor!

The teacher was furious, "Who did this?"

Everyone knew it was Mo.

But Man-Man wasn't going to let Mo know how upset she was. She wasn't going to cry or make a fuss. She quickly stood up and moved her seat back. Then she began to write in her little notebook.

So it began: the war between Mo and Man-Man.

WAR

There was a war every day between Mo and Man-Man.

It was usually Mo who started it but Man-Man always fought back.

In Maths, the Maths teacher asked them to finish 100 Maths problems every day. If someone got even one answer wrong, he or she had to do ten extra problems as a punishment. Mo kept getting things wrong, so he always had loads of extra problems to do. He'd had enough!

Man-Man never got a single answer wrong. So Mo

had an idea! He decided he would copy her answers. Every time he finished a problem, he snuck a look at Man-Man's notebook to see what *she'd* written. If he didn't have the same answer, Mo corrected it right away.

One day, Mo got all 100 problems right: 100 out of 100 – a perfect score! The Maths teacher was really pleased. Mo even got a star in his notebook.

The teacher told the class that if you try hard enough, you can do anything. He said Mo had tried really hard that day with his Maths problems, and he had succeeded.

Mo usually got told off all the time so getting this praise from the teacher made him feel pretty good! He looked at Man-Man's notebook and saw that she'd got 100 too. But she hadn't got a star!

Mo picked up Man-Man's Maths notebook and said loudly, "Man-Man, where's your star?"

Man-Man snatched her book back and said, "You only got that star because you copied my answers."

"What do you mean? What proof have you got?" said Mo.

Man-Man had no proof. Mo had won that particular battle...

But the next day, when they were given their Maths problems, Man-Man deliberately wrote wrong answers to more than half of the problems! She wasn't going to let Mo get away with it again.

Mo had finished his problems and he looked over to compare his answers to Man-Man's. He had never had SO many wrong answers! He couldn't understand it. He quickly rubbed out his answers and copied Man-Man's

Man-Man waited until Mo had rubbed out his answers and copied down hers; then she immediately rubbed out her wrong answers and wrote down the correct ones!

Mo had no idea that Man-Man had played a trick on him. He was still daydreaming about getting another star in his notebook.

The next day in Maths class, the teacher walked into the classroom looking FURIOUS. He looked at Mo sternly. Mo's heart started to thump loudly, what had he done?

"Mo! Come here, please," said the Maths teacher.

The teacher showed Mo his Maths note book. Mo took one look. The notebook was full of red Xs.

"Mo, yesterday I said you had improved. How do

you explain all these wrong answers? You got 53 wrong out of 100!"

The Maths teacher went on and on, but Mo didn't hear a word. What had gone wrong?

Mo kept on thinking about one thing. *If I got 53 answers wrong, how many wrong answers did Man-Man get?*

It was driving Mo nuts. He had to find out.

Mo gathered up his courage and asked, in a quiet voice, "How many answers did Man-Man get wrong?"

The Maths teacher took out Man-Man's notebook. Mo took one look and saw that it was full of red ticks, that the mark was 100/100!

No way! Mo *knew* he'd compared his answers with Man-Man's yesterday. How had he got 53 answers wrong, but Man-Man had got them all right? The Maths teacher must have made a mistake when he was marking the notebooks.

Mo blurted out to the teacher, "Are you sure you didn't make a mistake when you marked the problems?"

The teacher EXPLODED. Then he gave ten new problems for every one Mo had got wrong. That was 530 problems to do for homework. It wasn't FAIR.

Mo had learned his lesson the hard way, but it was a lesson he would never forget. From that day on, every time Mo did Maths problems, he would think of that nightmarish day. He would never be careless again. He would never compare answers with Man-Man again. And he would *never* be tricked by Man-Man... again.

PATIENT MAN-MAN

Man-Man was Little Miss Perfect. She never forgot to do her homework. She never made a mistake with her writing and had to cross something out.

Mo's writing had more scribbles and crossings out than words!

Man-Man could recite poetry on demand. She never came to school with scuffed shoes, or uncombed hair. And she was never, ever late for school. But one day, she wasn't in the playground when the bell rang.

Mo longed for Man-Man to do something that wasn't

perfect. Whenever Mo found something Man-Man had done wrong, he felt a whole lot better about himself.

By the end of morning playtime, Man-Man had still not arrived at school.

Mo decided she must be playing truant!

"Ms Qin! Ms Qin!" Mo rushed to Ms Qin's office making a big fuss as if there was a fire drill, "Man-Man is truanting!"

"What are you talking about?" Ms Qin gave Mo a warning look. "Man-Man is ill today, her mother called to tell me."

"What? Man-Man's ill?" Mo repeated.

However much he hated Man-Man bossing him around and her being right all the time, Mo remembered the days when he had liked Man-Man. And, though he was always getting into trouble, Mo was a kind and caring boy. What was the matter with Man-Man? Did she have a bad tummy? Did she have a temperature?

"Ms Qin, shall I go and see Man-Man after school?"

"That's a very kind and responsible offer," said Ms Qin. "But you can't go on your own. Lily and Wen have also offered to go, so the three of you can go to Man-Man's house together."

Ms Qin went on saying something else, but Mo wasn't paying attention. For the first time in his life, Ms Qin had called him "kind and responsible" instead of going on about his mischief making!

When school was over, Mo didn't go home with Hippo, Monkey and Penguin as usual. He saw Lily and Wen walking together, and he caught up.

"Wait for me! I'm coming too!"

Lily didn't know what Mo wanted.

"Ms Qin said I can come and see Man-Man with you. She said I was being *kind* and *responsible*."

"You? RESPONSIBLE?" Wen sneered. "You must be joking!"

"If you don't believe me, just go ask Ms Qin."

"OK," Wen said hesitatingly, "I believe you. But if you come and see Man-Man, you might make her feel worse."

"Why?"

"Because Man-Man gets cross whenever she sees you."

"That's not FAIR," said Mo. "It's only because—"

"Oh, stop it, you two," Lily interrupted. "Come on or we'll never get there."

"I think we should buy Man-Man a get-well present," said Mo.

"I haven't got any money on me," Wen said, quickly.

Mo knew that Wen *did* have money on him. His money was inside his underpants. Wen's mum had sewn a secret pocket in all his underpants to put money inside. Mo had noticed a pocket once when they were changing for PE. But he thought he'd better not say anything.

"I've got three Yuan," Lily said.

"I've got six Yuan," Mo said.

Mo had been planning to spend his pocket money on a new comic book.

"Let's use the money we've got to buy Man-Man some flowers," Lily said.

"Flowers are boring," replied Mo. "They're just eye-candy, you can only look at them. Let's buy Man-Man something yummy to eat."

Mo thought that if he was ill, he'd want food, not flowers.

But Lily thought that if she was ill, she'd want flowers and not food! Food might make her feel worse.

They couldn't agree.

In the end, Lily bought a small bunch of blue

chrysanthemums from the florist and Mo bought a bag of freshly-baked chocolate-walnut cookies from the bakery.

When they got to Man-Man's house, Lily gave Man-Man the bunch of blue chrysanthemums.

"Oh thank you, they're so pretty! Blue is my favourite colour," Man-Man exclaimed.

Mo gave Man-Man the bag of delicious chocolate-walnut cookies.

"Thank you. You can put them on the table!" That was all she said.

Lily gave Mo a victory smile as if to say, "Ha! Man-Man liked my chrysanthemums better than your cookies."

But Man-Man *did* like the cookies! They smelled wonderful, and she wanted to eat them. She just wasn't going to let Mo know that. She had to pretend that she wasn't hungry. She would only eat them after Mo had left.

"Mo, what are you doing here?" she demanded.

"Ms Qin said I could come. She said I was being kind and *responsible*."

Man-Man felt a battle coming on. She couldn't stop herself from wanting to boss Mo around whenever she was with him.

"Mo, have you learned those two poems yet? We have to recite them tomorrow in class. So recite them to me, if you can remember them."

Mo had thought that since Man-Man was sick, he wouldn't have to recite the poems. Mo *hated* poems. And even more than he hated poems, he hated reciting them!

"Man-Man, you're ill. Do you really want me to recite poetry?"

"I most certainly do!" Man-Man replied.

It was funny how only a minute ago Man-Man had been acting like she was really ill, but now she seemed to be better and was bossing Mo around.

Man-Man saw that Mo didn't want to recite the poems, so she asked Lily to pass her rucksack from the table.

"What do you need that for?" Lily asked.

"I need my notebook – the one I use to keep track of Mo's Mischief. I'm going to note down that he wouldn't recite the poems."

Mo saw the notebook coming out, so he quickly changed his mind. "All right, all right, I'll recite them!"

Mo recited the poems once. Man-Man said he had made two mistakes.

Mo recited the poems again. Man-Man said he hadn't put any *feeling* into them.

So Mo recited the poems a third time. This time he put a whole load of dramatic *feeling* into them – he even did actions. Lily and Wen started to giggle at Mo's gestures. Man-Man put her hand to her mouth. She was *not* going to laugh. At the end of his recitation, Mo did a great sweeping bow. Man-Man couldn't hold it anymore. She burst out laughing.

Mo was fed up. He'd done his best and the others were laughing at him. He wanted to go home, right now. Just as he was about to storm out, Man-Man's grandmother came into the room. She had heard the laughter and wanted to thank Mo for making Man-Man better. She asked Mo to stay for tea.

Who would believe it? Before Mo had come to visit, Man-Man had been really ill. But once Mo was there, all Man-Man could think about was bossing him about! She had forgotten all about being ill. She was better!

Man-Man's grandmother said that Mo was like a magic pill, and he must stay for tea otherwise she would be very upset. Mo had no choice.

MO, THE MAGIC PILL

Man-Man wasn't very happy that Grandma had asked Mo to stay for tea. She didn't want to sit at the table with that annoying boy. So she invited Lily and Wen to stay as well. Grandma wasn't pleased about *that*: Wen and Lily weren't the children who had made her granddaughter better!

While they were waiting for tea, Wen and Lily might as well have not been there. Man-Man just kept on at Mo all the time. Another battle was about to begin!

Mo was just going through Man-Man's bookshelf

looking for comic books (which were the only books Mo was interested in). Man-Man yelled at him.

"Mo, don't touch any of my things without permission!"

Mo jumped. He looked around Man-Man's room for anything interesting, and was just about to sit on Man-Man's bed.

"Mo, don't sit on my bed!" Man-Man yelled again.

"Then where am I supposed to sit?"

Man-Man pointed to a chair by the door. "Over there. You can go and sit over there."

"Fine." Mo sat on the chair by the door feeling like a prisoner. He didn't even know where to put his hands and feet.

Finally, Mo felt that he had had enough, and stood up abruptly.

"Where do you think you're going?" Man-Man asked.

"I'm going home!"

"No, you're not!" Man-Man raised her voice. "My grandma asked you to stay for tea!"

Man-Man didn't seem to be ill anymore. If she was ill, she wouldn't have so much energy. If she was ill, she wouldn't be able to shout so loudly!

Man-Man's grandmother rushed out of the kitchen when she heard the ruckus. "Mo, you can't leave. If you stay, my dear little Man-Man will feel so much better!"

"But she just bosses me around!" Mo complained.

"Then let her boss you around!" Lily whispered in Mo's ear. "Just pretend you're the doctor, and that you're in charge!"

Mo giggled. He didn't know Lily could be funny.

"Mo, if you really want to leave, you must leave." Wen didn't like seeing Lily whispering to Mo. He wanted Mo to go away.

"I don't think Mo should leave," Man-Man's grandmother said, firmly. Man-Man's grandmother didn't like Wen – he was far too big for his boots.

"Mo, dear, you must be hungry. Why don't you eat some of these chocolate walnut cookies." Man-Man's grandmother patted Mo's head. She didn't know the cookies were a get-well present from Mo to Man-Man.

Man-Man's grandma handed a cookie to Mo. Just as Mo was about to take a bite, Man-Man yelled at him again. "You can't eat the cookie without washing your hands first!"

Mo was startled and he dropped the cookie. It

broke into pieces and there were crumbs all over the floor!

Man-Man jumped out of bed. She showed Mo the bathroom, and told him to wash his hands with soap *three* times and rinse *three* times.

Mo's patience was wearing thin. He had to think of a way to get his own back...

"Now you may eat the cookie," said Man-Man, firmly.

Mo was really hungry by now. He quickly shoved down the chocolate walnut cookie. It tasted delicious! The cookie was really crispy, and Mo chewed loudly as he gobbled it down.

"Mo!" Man-Man started again, "Don't you know? You're not supposed to eat your food so loudly."

"Why not?" Mo was starting to lose patience. Why did Man-Man have to boss him around on everything, even eating?

"Only pigs eat like that!"

"Fine! I won't eat them then! Are you happy?" Mo was about to lose his temper.

"No, I'm not. You *have* to eat them!" Man-Man wasn't going to let Mo off the hook. "AND you mustn't make that noise when you eat."

"Fine!" He would be a fool not to eat them. The chocolate walnut cookies tasted so good.

But Mo didn't dare to chew this time – instead, he ground the cookies down with his teeth. But the cookies were just too crispy, and Mo couldn't help but make a little noise.

"I heard that! Try again!"

"Fine!" He would be a fool to refuse. The cookies tasted absolutely *amazing*.

Mo had an idea. He ate another cookie. This time, he chewed really loudly on purpose.

"Why are you chewing *more* loudly now?"

"I wasn't," said Mo craftily. "But if you insist, I'll try again with another cookie!"

Wen saw through Mo's little trick. "Wait a minute!" he exclaimed. "The cookies will all be gone if you keep on eating them."

There had only been eight chocolate walnut cookies in the bag. Mo had just eaten six of them, and one had fallen on the ground. So now there was only one cookie left…

By now, Man-Man's room was filled with a lovely chocolatey smell of cookies. Wen was almost drooling over the smell. Man-Man was desperate to try one too. Only Lily didn't look interested. She never ate sweet things, since she was always careful to keep fit for her ballet lessons. But Lily was enjoying watching Mo eating. He was so funny! And she was enjoying the battle between him and Man-Man...

"Let him eat," Lily said. "I'm sure he won't make any noise this time. Right, Mo?"

Mo didn't make any noise when he ate the last cookie, but not because he wanted to obey Man-Man. He wanted to impress Lily. Instead of chewing and grinding, Mo let the cookie stay in his mouth until it slowly melted – it was DIVINE.

The battle was over. Mo had won again

Just then, Man-Man's parents came back from work. They were quite surprised when they saw how rosy-cheeked Man-Man was. "Man-Man, are you feeling better now?"

"Yes, she's cured!" Man-Man's grandma smiled. "She felt better the moment Mo came!"

"Which one of you is Mo?" Man-Man's parents asked.

Man-Man's parents knew the name Mo Shen Ma very well. Man-Man was always telling them what a mischievous and naughty boy he was.

Mo bowed formally and respectfully to Man-Man's father. "Nice to meet you, Mr Man-Man!"

Then, Mo bowed formally and respectfully to Man-Man's mother. "Nice to meet you, Mrs Man-Man!"

"What a *charming* boy!" they both said.

Man-Man wanted to introduce Wen to her parents. "Wen is the brainiest in our class; he loves to work on difficult problems, and he—"

Man-Man went on and on about how brilliant Wen was, so that her parents would stop being interested in Mo. But it didn't work. Man-Man's parents invited Mo to sit in the place of honour at the head of the table.

Mo had never been treated so well in all his life! It went to his head a little bit. He ignored Man-Man's angry glances and started showing off. But when he saw all the food on the table, Mo got a little quieter. He had eaten seven chocolate walnut cookies already, now he had to eat all of Man-Man's Grandma's tea! Was Mo about to get into a new battle?

TEAM PLAY

Mo and his friends were now in Year Four and this meant they would have a very special treat. In the summer term, all the Year Fours went on a picnic. But it wasn't any ordinary picnic – this was a picnic where the children had to cook their own food!

Mo felt more excited about this trip than about the Spring Festival or even his birthday. For the last few nights he'd been too excited to get to sleep. When he couldn't sleep, he would go into the kitchen and dig around to see what sort of things he could take to the picnic.

Mo hoped Ms Qin would talk about the picnic in class. But she didn't say anything about it for days. Finally, one Tuesday afternoon, Ms Qin *had* to talk to the class about the picnic. If she didn't, there wouldn't be enough time to get everything organised.

"You can each choose your own teams," said Ms Qin. "But there must be eight children in each team; four boys and four girls."

"Yes!" Mo exclaimed happily. This was exactly what he wanted.

Ms Qin went on. "For the picnic, every team can cook whatever they want."

"Yes!" Mo beamed with joy, because this was *exactly* what he wanted too.

Ms Qin carried on. "At the picnic, there will be a competition. Every team will compete. There'll be a prize for the team that cooks the best food. Some of you will be judges and will have the responsibility of choosing the winners!"

"YES!" For the third time, Mo was ecstatic. He really wanted to be a judge, so that he could try every team's food.

When Ms Qin was finally finished, Mo, Hippo, Monkey and Penguin immediately got together. The four of them were best friends and always hung out together; the four of them *had* to be on the same team. They were absolutely *not* to be separated. So, there were four boys – now they needed to find four girls for their team.

"Let's ask Lily to be in our team," Penguin said.

Penguin wanted Lily in their team, because as a ballet dancer, Lily wouldn't eat much. So Penguin could eat her share as well as his own!

The other three boys agreed. Lily was the prettiest girl in the class. If their team had the prettiest girl in the class, it would make all of them look good. But the boys weren't sure whether Lily would want to join their team. She was a bit of a stuck-up princess. When she walked, she always kept her chin up, and she *never* talked to the boys. But Penguin told them not to worry and that he would handle everything.

Being Lily's desk-mate, Penguin knew that Lily was not really stuck-up at all. She only walked with her chin up because she was a ballet dancer. She only looked straight ahead instead of sideways because she liked to think she was performing on the stage!

The four boys went to look for Lily.

Lily was talking to Man-Man. Man-Man wanted Lily to be in *her* team.

"Hey, Lily," Penguin said matter-of-factly. "Come and join our team."

Before Lily had the chance to reply, "No, she's going to be in *my* team."

"In that case, let's ask someone else," Mo said, quickly

"Mo!" Man-Man started yelling, "You *have to* be in my team as well."

"What? No way! Ms Qin said we could choose our own teams. I'm *no*t going to be in yours."

"But Ms Qin said I had to keep an eye on you. How can I do that if we're not in the same team?"

"Lily will keep an eye on me. I don't mind her doing that because she is SO pretty." Mo said this on purpose to upset Man-Man…

"Mo! How… how could you…"

Man-Man was upset. She wanted to Mo to think that *she* was the prettiest! She grabbed her notebook so she could write down this latest piece of mischief…

"Hold on a minute, Man-Man," Penguin said. He grabbed Mo and whispered, "Lily's already agreed to be on Man-Man's team – we have no choice but to ask Man-Man to team up with us."

Monkey joined in. "If we don't let Man-Man boss you around, Man-Man will take Lily away from us, that's for sure."

Hippo really wanted Lily to be on their team. She was so pretty! "Mo, lets just team up with Man-Man! What does it matter?"

"All right, let's do it." Mo had been forced to team up with his arch-enemy, Man-Man!

So Mo's team now had six members for the picnic: four boys and two girls. They needed to find two more girls.

"How about Angel?" Hippo said.

Hippo thought Angel was a good choice because Angel was fun, and she never got into trouble.

Everyone agreed except Mo. Man-Man and Lily were quite happy to have Angel on their team. Angel wasn't particularly clever, or particularly pretty. Man-Man and Lily thought that they would look even cleverer and prettier than usual if Angel hung out with them.

"Why don't you want Angel on the team, Mo?" Penguin grinned at Mo as if he knew something. "I thought you two were quite close."

Great. That was the one thing Mo didn't want to hear. Angel was Mo's neighbour, she was the girl Mo hung out most of the time. Mo wouldn't mind people saying they were *close*, if Angel was half as pretty as Lily, or half as clever as Man-Man! He was a bit embarrassed to be friends with her, to be honest. But Angel *was* his friend and he liked her. So he agreed.

The seven of them only had to find one more girl.

All of them thought of Joy. Joy travelled to school each day from the countryside, and was Angel's best friend at school. Best friends should be together, so if Angel was on their team, Joy should also be on their team.

Again, both Man-Man and Lily were happy to have Joy in their team. They were sure that Joy wouldn't outshine either of them, since she wore old-fashioned clothes and was a bit timid.

Man-Man was the first to find Angel and Joy. "We've decided that you two are in our team," Man-Man said it in such a bossy way that the two girls didn't dare say no. And they didn't want to say no, anyway. Angel and Joy were really happy to be chosen. Man-Man had never taken any notice of them before. She always acted so superior. They couldn't understand why she had asked them to be in her team.

Later on, Penguin told the two girls that it was Mo who had *particularly* wanted Angel in his team! Angel beamed when she heard this. Good job she didn't know the real reason...

TEAM LEADER

So now the team was complete. The four boys were Mo, Hippo, Monkey and Penguin. The four girls were Man-Man, Lily, Angel and Joy.

All the teams had to stay after school to hold their first meeting about the picnic. This was a very important meeting and everything that was discussed had to be kept secret from the other teams. They were going to decide on what to cook at the picnic. This really mattered because the teams were competing for the Best Cooking prize. What each team decided to cook had to be TOP SECRET!

Mo wanted to find a secret meeting place so no one else could get wind of their plans. He stalked around the playground like a detective following a lead. He found the perfect spot behind the boys' toilets where there were some blackberry bushes. Not only could they meet in secret, they could eat the blackberries too!

"What do you think of this place?" Mo asked proudly, "Can't get more secret than this... or more juicy."

"What a horrible choice." Man-Man had to disagree with Mo every single time. "There is a *raspberry* bush behind the girls' toilets. Raspberries are *much* nicer than blackberries. Why don't we go there?"

Oh dear. The two of them were arguing again.

Lily said, "Let's forget about both the boys' and the girl's toilets, and about the blackberries and the raspberries. Let's choose *another* meeting spot."

"I know somewhere," Monkey said. "It's nice. It's a

very secret spot where children don't go."

Everyone was curious, but Monkey wouldn't tell them more. "Follow me," he said.

Monkey jogged towards the place he had in mind. It wasn't in the playground. It wasn't in the school grounds at all! When the place was almost in sight, Mo, Hippo and Penguin started to realize where they were going. There it was: a tiny but luxurious building with glazed tiles, which gave off a dazzling glow in the sunlight. It was… a public toilet!

It was hidden discreetly behind a thick canopy of trees, a place where the boys often hung out when they were up to mischief.

"I'm not sure we should be here…" Lily said.

Monkey pointed towards the thick canopy of trees that shielded the public toilets from view. "But it's so secret!"

Monkey was right. This *was* a secret place; so secret that only people who really needed the toilet would ever come here!

"Fine! Let's start the meeting, then." Man-Man knew that once Monkey started talking, he wouldn't stop for hours. They needed to get on with it.

"Wait a minute!" Mo suddenly thought of something

worth arguing with Man-Man about. "We haven't got a team leader. We MUST elect a team leader first."

Everyone, except Mo, assumed that Man-Man would be their team leader for the picnic. Mo didn't really care who the team leader was, but he really didn't want to be bossed around by Man-Man.

"We all decided who should be in our team, so we should all decide who will be our team leader. We have to have an election," Mo insisted.

"Fine, we'll just see who *everyone* chooses to be the team leader then!" Man-Man said, grumpily.

Mo started drumming up support for himself. "Hey, guys, you should all elect me to be your team leader. I can *guarantee* that our team will defeat all the other teams in the Best Cooking competition."

"OK, Mo, I'll vote for you!" Angel said. Angel still thought that Mo had specially asked for her to be included in the team...

"All right! One vote for me!" Mo shouted, triumphantly. "Who else will vote for me? Lily, how about you?"

Lily thought Mo was funny. She remembered the cookies he'd eaten when Man-Man was ill. He also

seemed to be the most enthusiastic member of the team so she nodded and said, "OK, I'll vote for you."

Because Lily had voted for Mo, Penguin voted for him too. And because Penguin had voted for Mo, so did Hippo and Monkey.

Angel had voted for Mo, so her best-friend Joy did the same. Secretly, everyone except Man-Man thought that Mo would be the most fun to have as their team leader.

So, Man-Man had to give in. But she was really upset because her best-friend had voted for her enemy. If best friends didn't vote for each other, why should they stay best friends?

Lily had no idea that she'd made Man-Man really upset. She walked towards Man-Man and whispered, "Just let Mo be the team leader for now. After the picnic is over, he'll go straight back to being nobody again."

Man-Man thought that this was probably true, so she felt a bit better.

"Order. Order. This meeting is in session!" Mo shouted.

Mo had never been the leader of anything in his life before. Although being the team leader for a picnic really wasn't that big a deal, it was still important. Mo decided he would be a good and fair leader.

First things first, Mo cleared his throat and decided to give a speech. "I am very honoured to have been elected your team leader for the picnic event. Why did you vote for me? Well, there are a number of reasons—"

"Mr Mo, let's skip the *reasons*," said Monkey.

"OK, we'll skip the reasons. Then let me tell you when the picnic will be—"

"Let's skip that too. Ms Qin already told us when the picnic is being held." Penguin was getting very impatient.

"Then … what shall I talk about?"

"Mr Mo, why don't you talk about what we should cook?" said Angel.

Angel was the only one who was patient with Mo. Mo had chosen her, after all. Now that Mo had been elected the team leader, Angel worshipped him even more.

Mo accepted Angel's suggestion. "OK, let me tell you what we should cook on the picnic day."

"That should be decided by everyone on the team," said Man-Man.

"Oh, no," Mo groaned to himself. Who would have known it would be so hard to be a leader? Mo backed off and said, "Fine, why don't you suggest something first!"

"I suggest we make dumplings."

Everyone objected. They thought dumplings were too boring.

"Why don't we make vegetable sticks and fruit salad?" Lily said.

Again, everyone objected. Vegetable sticks and fruit salad might be healthy, but they'd all be starving if that was all they had to eat.

There were many more suggestions but they couldn't agree on any of them. All the team members were out of ideas... but their leader hadn't spoken yet.

"Mr Mo, why don't *you* suggest something?" Angel said sweetly.

Mo had made up his mind about what he wanted to cook ages ago. But since he was the leader, he had to listen to what everyone else had to say first, and then make the final decision.

"We shall make spicy meat and vegetable shish-kebabs!"

And that was that!

BEING BOSS

On Thursday morning, all the Year Fours were waiting to get on the bus that would take them to the countryside for the picnic.

The playground was bustling with children carrying pots and pans, and food and drink cartons, making the whole place look like a café. Mo's team was the only one that didn't have pots and pans. Instead, Mo and Penguin carried a bundle of steel pipes, and Hippo and Monkey carried a box. Man-Man, Lily, Angel and Joy followed behind carrying bags of meat and vegetables.

Wen pointed to the pipes Mo was carrying. "We're supposed to be cooking, not plumbing," he sneered.

Mo shouted, "MYOB!" and started to walk away, but Wen carried on taunting him.

"Mo, we're going for a picnic, not to fix someone's sink!"

Wen was the only one cracking up at his own joke. No one else laughed.

Other children in the playground were longing to know what the steel pipes were for. But no one in Mo's team would tell them, because they didn't want to give away their secret. Besides, their leader – Mr Mo – had given them STRICT ORDERS. The *spicy meat and vegetable shish-kebab* plan must remain TOP SECRET before the picnic!

Someone in the class must have told Ms Qin that Mo's team was taking bundles of steel pipes to the picnic instead of pots and pans. Ms Qin was a little worried... and a little suspicious. What kind of mischief was Mo up to now? She started regretting having given Mo permission to be a team leader.

"Mo, where are your pots and pans?" asked Ms Qin.

"We don't need pots and pans for our picnic," Mo said.

"But how are you going to cook food then?"

"We just don't need them, I promise." Mo was determined to keep their plan a secret.

Ms Qin saw that other members of Mo's hadn't got pots and pans either, and nor did they have bowls, chopsticks or spoons.

"No pots and pans, not even bowls and chopsticks! Don't tell me you're going to eat with your hands like cavemen!" Ms Qin was getting *really* worried.

Man-Man was the only one who could stop Ms Qin from worrying, because Ms Qin always trusted what Man-Man said.

"Ms Qin, please believe me, everything is under control."

Man-Man's words put Ms Qin at ease. *The boys in Mo's team are so naughty, they're always getting into trouble. Thank goodness Man-Man is in the same team!* Ms Qin thought.

When they arrived at the picnic area, all the stoves were laid out in a row. Ms Qin wanted to give a stove to Mo's team, but Mo said they didn't need one.

"You don't need fire either? You really are going to eat like cavemen then!" Ms Qin wasn't sure whether to laugh or cry.

All the other teams began to prepare for cooking. Mo was really confident. He found an open area and began to untie the bundle of steel pipes with Hippo, Monkey and Penguin.

The steel pipes were going to be turned into a barbecue grill. Mo had brought these pipes from home. His father was the head of a toy factory. He loved to invent new toys and he also loved to eat good food. So Mo's house was full of toys... and kitchen gadgets.

Mo easily fitted the pipes together to make a barbecue grill.

The barbecue grill was ready and now Mo began to give jobs to the team members.

"Since I'm the team leader, you all have to do what I say. Is that clear?" he said.

"Show off," Penguin murmured.

"Penguin! I can't hear you, why don't you repeat that a bit louder?"

"Mr Mo, if we don't start cooking, we'll fall behind the other teams," Man-Man said.

Mo knew that Man-Man was being sarcastic when she called him Mr Mo. Hmph! He decided to give her the hardest and messiest job…

"Man-Man, you will be responsible for washing the vegetables. You have to make sure the vegetables are squeaky clean, so you'll need to wash them at least eight times."

Though Man-Man didn't say anything, she gave Mo an angry stare and started to work.

Lily wanted to help Man-Man out but Mo wouldn't let her. Mo wanted to give the easiest job to Lily so that she might want to sit next to him when they got back to school. But he had to think about what the easiest job might be, so he gave out the other jobs first.

"Joy, you will be in charge of cutting the meat and

vegetables. Angel, you will use the bamboo sticks to skewer the meat and vegetables."

"Mo, what do you want *me* to do?" Lily asked.

Mo couldn't be feeling better. He loved being in charge. Even someone as stuck-up as Lily was begging for work to do!

"Mo, Lily's talking to you!" Hippo shouted at Mo. He couldn't stand Mo acting so big in front of Lily.

Hippo's voice brought Mo back to reality. "Lily, after Angel finishes skewering the shish-kebabs, you can bring them to the grill."

"That's too easy!" moaned Lily. She asked Mo to give her something more difficult.

Mo didn't often get the chance to talk to Lily, so he was going to make the most of this opportunity. "Lily, bringing the shish-kebabs to the barbecue is a *skilled* job. You have to have good balance to do it. Otherwise the kebabs might fall on the ground. With your ballet training, you're the best person for the job."

"Mo, you are so full of nonsense!" Penguin was losing patience again. "Hurry up and give me a job!"

Mo was annoyed. Why did Penguin have to cut off his conversation with Lily? He deserved to give Penguin the worst job! "You can be in charge of the grill then! And Hippo, you can be in charge of barbecuing!"

"Mo, what about me? What about me?" Monkey asked anxiously.

"You will be the assistant."

"But what will I do?" Monkey was confused.

"You will do all the little things, helping where help is needed," Mo said.

Monkey wasn't happy about being the assistant, so he asked Mo what job he was giving himself.

"I am the Commander-in-Chief."

Mo straightened himself up and said, smugly; "The Commander-in-Chief gives the orders. Others do the work."

THE COOKING
BATTLES

Mo had made himself Commander-in-Chief and was determined not to do any of the work. While his team members worked really hard, Mo just walked around leisurely, bossing everyone around.

"Man-Man, I see some dark spots on those lotus roots. Go and wash them again."

Mo was nit-picking, just as Man-Man used to do with him. She had already washed the lotus roots squeaky clean, but Mo picked each one up and inspected them carefully.

"The dark spots are natural, you can't wash them off," Man-Man argued.

"I am the team leader. If I say they're not clean, they're not clean."

Mo smiled as Man-Man started washing the roots again. He couldn't believe it. He was actually bossing Man-Man around and she was doing as he told her!

"Penguin, what are you doing?" Mo barked.

"Can't you see what I'm doing?" moaned Penguin, crossly.

Penguin was looking hot and bothered. He was trying to fan the fire with a sheet of newspaper. But instead of getting a flame going, there was only black smoke coming out.

"Come on! Fan harder!" Mo said loudly.

"No, No. Don't fan too hard!" said Joy. "Stop giving nonsense orders, Mo," she pleaded.

Joy walked over to the barbecue, picked up an iron stick and poked around the charcoals a little bit. Then she fanned it gently. Magically, a blue flame appeared.

"Incredible! Amazing!" Penguin dropped one knee to the ground, bowed respectfully to Joy and said,

"Master Joy, please may I be your pupil!"

Joy went bright red. She blushed to the roots of her hair. She told everyone that because she came from the countryside, she had learned how to light a fire and cook meals in the open air when she was really young.

Joy was also good at her job. She made two chef's hats out of newspapers for Penguin and Hippo, since they were in charge of the barbecuing.

Mo thought the hats were great, so he gave the order for Joy to make all the team members one.

"Do girls have to wear the hats too?" Angel asked.

"Of course!" Mo made a commanding gesture, "We must all have the same uniform!"

Just then, Mo saw that the shish-kebab sticks Angel had skewered were a bit uneven. Some had too many pieces of meat on them, while others had almost none.

"Angel, you're not counting properly. Skewer them again; eight pieces of meat on each stick, no more, no less."

Angel obeyed Mo's orders – she would do anything he asked. She re-skewered the shish-kebabs while counting, eight pieces of meat, no more, no less.

Lily carried the skewers that were ready to be barbecued to Hippo.

Mo was the only one on the team who knew how to barbecue like this. His father had shown him what to do last summer. He recited the five barbecue rules to everyone.

"Step Number One: Brush on a layer of cooking oil.

Step Number Two: Sprinkle some salt.

Step Number Three: Brush a layer of shish-kebab sauce.

Step Number Four: Add hot pepper powder.

Step Number Five: Sprinkle on some Chinese prickly ash... and it's ready to serve!

Remember, you must keep on brushing and keep on twisting and turning the skewers when you barbecue," Mo explained to Hippo.

"I need more than two hands for all that!"

Mo suddenly thought of Monkey. He hadn't seen him around for a while. As Monkey was the assistant, he should be assisting.

"Monkey! Where is Monkey?" Mo called out.

"Mr Mo. Here I am." Monkey appeared out of nowhere.

Mo was suspicious. "What are you doing sneaking around?" he asked.

"I was spying on the other teams. I have a very

important piece of information to report: we have a rival for the Best Cooking prize."

"Who?"

"Wen's team," Monkey said, "They're making pizza!"

"What makes them think they can make pizza?"

"Wen's team said they are making authentic Italian pizza, and they said it will be much better than our spicy shish-kebabs."

"Well, they can dream on, no one will beat our spicy shish-kebabs!"

Although Mo sounded confident, he felt a little sick. Everyone loved pizza. He needed to see if Wen's team really was their main rival. He casually strolled over to Wen's picnic area...

"Are you here to see a master at work, Mo?" asked Wen. "Would you like to learn from me how to make authentic Italian Pizza in the Chinese countryside?"

"Let me see if they're any good, then I'll decide whether to learn from you or not," Mo said arrogantly.

Wen started to demonstrate his pizza-making skills. He patted and rolled a piece of pizza dough into a circle. Then he placed the dough into a flat pan, and put diced ham, pepper, pineapple, mushroom and tomato on top of the dough.

Mo laughed when he saw what Wen was doing. "Wen, do you really think that's how you make Italian pizza? You'll never make pizza that way. Do you want to know why?"

Wen did want to know why. But he'd never admit that to Mo.

Mo carried on "Let me tell you something. To make *authentic* Italian pizza, you need two things: first, you need Italian cheese which goes on top of the dough; second, you need a fire oven that's as big as a little house. A *wood* fire. *Authentic* Italian pizza is made by baking it in an oven, not by grilling it in a flat pan. You haven't got cheese or a fire oven as big as a little house. Your pizza won't work!"

Wen couldn't believe what he'd just heard. He hadn't realised that Mo – silly, naughty Mo – could possibly know so much about anything, let alone making authentic Italian pizza. He didn't know that Mo had learned everything he just said from Penguin.

Penguin and his parents had once taken Mo out to an Italian pizza restaurant. Penguin's father told Mo why Italian pizza is unique. The boys were shown the oven that was as big as a little house. The Italian chef who made the pizza was as big and tall as a tower. The chef even taught Penguin and Mo how to use the long spade to put pizza into the oven.

So Mo was finally able to teach Wen a lesson.

Just as Mo was having the time of his life, Man-Man yelled out, "Mo! We're all busy working, and you're not doing ANYTHING. It's not fair!"

"I'm the team leader. The Commander-in-Chief. You can't boss me around."

"Of course I can boss you around! Ms Qin asked me to keep an eye on you."

There was about to be another battle, but then—

There was a sudden breeze, and with it came a mouth-watering smell!

Mo took a deep breath. "Our spicy shish-kebabs are ready, everyone!"

MOUTH-WATERING SPICY SHISH-KEBABS

As soon as Mo smelled the mouth-watering aroma of spicy shish-kebab, he ran back to his team, ignoring Man-Man, who was still trying boss him around.

On the grill, the shish-kebabs were a deep golden brown. Sprinkled with pepper powder, Chinese prickly ash, and the *must-have* shish-kebab sauce, they looked rich, juicy... and DELICIOUS.

Mo had to stop himself from drooling over the

shish-kebabs. He asked Hippo whether they were ready to be eaten, but Hippo had no idea since he hadn't had the chance to taste them.

"Let me! Let me!" Penguin volunteered to try them out.

"No, I'm the team leader, so I shall try them!" Mo said. He told Penguin to keep on fanning the grill to keep the fire strong.

Mo picked up a meat shish-kebab. He was so desperate to try it that he bit a piece of meat off the stick without waiting for it to cool off. The meat was so hot that he had to roll it around on his tongue and ended up spitting it out.

"Is it done yet?" asked the others.

Penguin fanned the grill even faster while Hippo twisted and turned the shish-kebabs on the grill at incredible speed.

Mo had learned his lesson and this time he blew on the stick to cool it down before putting it inside his mouth.

"What's it like? What's it like?"

Everyone on the team gathered around.

"Zesty! Spicy! Tasty! It's delicious beyond words!" said Mo.

"Hooray! We did it! We're the champions!" they all shouted.

Mo's team cheered at a job well done, and rushed to try the freshly grilled shish-kebabs. They were all amazed at how good they tasted.

"This kebab is so tasty, I think my tongue is in heaven!" said Angel.

Mo saw there was one more cooked shish-kebab left, and was just about to go for it when Lily smacked at his hand.

"Wait a minute!" Lily said, "Hippo hasn't had one yet."

Hippo had been so busy twisting and turning the shish-kebabs on the grill that he hadn't even had a chance to take a break. Lily took the last cooked shish-kebab – the one she wouldn't let Mo have – and held it to Hippo's mouth. Hippo ate like a hippo, and in a split second, every single piece of meat on the stick was gone.

Mo patted Hippo on the shoulder. "Hey, Hippo, do you want me to take over the grilling for a while?"

"No, I'm all right," said Hippo. But his face was

flushed and sooty from the heat and smoke of the fire, and his forehead was a little bit sweaty.

"Aren't you tired?" said Mo.

"No, I'm not," replied Hippo.

Hippo's being a bit strange today, thought Mo. How could he not feel tired, even though he was working so hard? Was it because Lily was hanging around him as he worked? Was he showing off in front of her?

After Mo and his team had eaten enough meat kebabs, they tried roasting lotus roots, eggplants and bean curd.

Other teams were making wontons, dumplings, stir-fried vegetables and... pizza. But as the breeze carried the mouth-watering aroma of the grilled shish-kebabs to their picnic areas, they couldn't concentrate on what they were doing. The kebabs smelled so DELICIOUS that everyone wanted to try one.

No one knew who first sneaked over to Mo's team asking for a taste of their shish-kebabs. But news travelled fast about how wonderful the kebabs tasted. Soon, hordes of children were crowding around Mo's barbecue. As soon as a skewer of kebab was ready, it was served to a child in the queue.

"Line up! Line Up! Form one straight line!" Mo was really enjoying being in charge. "One skewer per person. No second servings!"

But every child who had tried one spicy shish-kebab wanted another! After finishing their first skewer, they went back into the queue and waited for another.

Nearly all the Year-Four children were gathered round Mo's barbecue by now. All of their own half-cooked food had been abandoned. There were dumplings scattered carelessly on the chopping boards; washed meat and vegetables in piles waiting to be fried; boiling wontons getting gooey and sticky...

Ms Qin couldn't understand it. What had Mo got up to this time?

Mo didn't look at the faces of the people in the queue, he was too busy. He handed a freshly grilled skewer of lotus roots to the next person and then noticed it wasn't a child. It was Ms Qin!

"Ms Qin, are you here to try our spicy shish-kebab too? Here, try the lotus roots, fresh from the grill!"

Ms Qin stared at Mo. The freshly grilled lotus roots

combined with the unique and zesty flavour of the kebab. How clever! Who could say no to such delicious food? Ms Qin couldn't resist trying a kebab.

Mo put on his sweetest voice and asked Ms Qin, "How do you like the taste?"

"I'd like another one, please, before I can answer!" Ms Qin said.

"One more order for Ms Qin!" Mo said loudly to his team.

But Lily ran over to Mo and said, "Mr Mo, we are out of food to grill!"

"What, there's nothing left?"

Mo was still hungry and so was everyone else on his team. They had been too busy barbecuing for everyone else to cook more for themselves.

"Our team has lots of vegetables, meat and fish. We haven't cooked them yet. Do you think you can grill those?" someone from another team asked Mo.

"As long as it's food, it can be grilled. Go and get it," he ordered

"Our team made some dumplings, can you grill dumplings?"

"As long as it's food, it can be grilled. Go get it!" he repeated.

"Wen's pizza tasted horrible and sour, can we grill it?"

"When we grill the pizza, the sourness will go!" Mo said confidently.

Every team brought their food over: some raw, some cooked, some half-cooked. It was all made into shish kebabs and grilled on Mo's barbecue grill.

Year Four had a feast. But Mo was still hungry. He had been much too busy being Commander-in-Chief. He commanded the class to grill and to eat. He didn't want to waste this valuable time as leader by doing something so boring as eating!

He knew that by the next day, everything would be back the way it was.

PRIZES

After every school trip, the class would discuss what was good and what was bad about the trip.

So the day after the school picnic, Ms Qin held a discussion with Year Four about the picnic event.

The children had already started calling the picnic "Mo's Barbecue".

But was the picnic a success? Ms Qin wondered. When it came to cooking, it was a bit of a disaster for every team except Mo's.

But does that make the picnic a disaster? wondered Ms Qin. Well, not only was no food wasted – not even

Wen's *authentic* Italian pizza – everyone in the class ate to their heart's content. Ms Qin had been teaching for almost thirty years. She had organised many picnic events, but no picnic had ever been like the one she experienced yesterday.

And it was all because of a boy called Mo!

Ms Qin decided to let the class decide how the picnic had gone.

First, she announced the winner of the Best Cooking prize. The spicy meat and vegetable shish-kebabs won!

"Hooray for Mo and his team!" everyone shouted... even Wen.

The cheer was deafening and the children stamped their feet on the floor. Mo stood up and waved at his classmates with a beaming smile.

"Mo, sit down!" Ms Qin frowned at Mo, she didn't want winning to go to his head. He was still full of mischief.

"Quiet! Quiet!" Ms Qin gestured to the class to calm down. "Although our barbecue team won the first prize, every child on that team worked hard to earn the prize. It wasn't the work of just *one* person."

Ms Qin threw a meaningful look at Mo.

Mo blushed. He wasn't feeling quite as smug now.

Ms Qin paused for a long time and then asked the class to discuss the picnic.

Several children put up their hands. Ms Qin picked Wen first.

"In my opinion, the success that the barbecue team had was mainly due to the fact that Lily and Man-Man were on the team."

Ms Qin smiled as Wen talked, so everyone thought that she agreed with him.

Mo refused to accept what Wen had just said. It was *him* who was the leader of the team! Without him they would never have won.

Then Lily stood up and said, "It was all thanks to Hippo that our team won the First Prize. Hippo did all the barbecuing."

That's not fair, thought Mo. He had taught Hippo how to barbecue shish-kebabs; he had brought the barbecue grill. Besides, the reason Hippo worked so hard was because Hippo had Lily as his partner, and that was thanks to Mo's excellent leadership skills!

Man-Man stood up and said, "We must also thank Joy and Angel who worked so hard yesterday to make this prize possible. And Penguin worked really hard too."

It seemed that everyone was being thanked except for the team leader! Mo was really fed up.

Angel had her hand up for a long time and was desperate to say something. Finally, Ms Qin called on her.

"It was Mo who had the *idea* of barbecuing spicy meat and vegetable shish-kebabs. We wouldn't have been able to win without Mo."

Mo felt better now. After Angel had finished speaking, everyone else who had their hands up put them down. It seemed that no one had anything else to say.

Apart from the Best Cooking prize, there was also the Best Team Leader prize. Again, the whole class put up their hands, keen to nominate their choice.

Ms Qin asked three children, and all three of them nominated Mo. This wasn't surprising. After all, who else deserved this prize better than Mo? The leader of the dumpling team? No. The leader of the dumpling team was the first to bring food to Mo's team to be barbecued. How about the leader of the wonton team? But the entire wonton team (including the leader) had abandoned their half-done wonton soup and went over to Mo's team to eat shish-kebabs. What about the leader of the Pizza team, Wen? Even the people on his team hadn't liked his sour-tasting pizza!

Wen stood up and said, "I don't think Mo should be awarded Best Team Leader. Ms Qin told us that the teams should all keep to their own areas and not go looking at what other teams were doing. But Mo wandered over to my team while we were cooking."

"Mo, did you wander over to Wen's team?" Ms Qin asked.

"Yes, but it was Monkey who *first* there. Monkey said Wen was going to make *authentic* Italian pizza, so I went over to take a look. But what they were making couldn't be further from *authentic* Italian pizza. To make *authentic* Italian pizza, you need to—"

Ms Qin quickly cut him off.

"Mo, it was against the rules to wander over to other teams while they were cooking."

"I don't agree that Mo should get the Best Team Leader prize, either." said Man-Man. "Ms Qin told us that the team leader should be a role model for others and join in the team effort. But all Mo did was wander around being bossy. He didn't *do* anything!"

"Mo, is this true?"

"But that's what team leaders do! They order people about," Mo said boldly.

The whole class burst out laughing.

Ms Qin was speechless. Mo was such a mischief maker, but here he was, being truly honest about himself. She had never been so unable to make up her mind before. Should she let Mo be elected the Best Team Leader?

"Let's vote, then!" Ms Qin thought this was the only way. "Raise your hand if you vote for Mo to get the Best Team Leader prize."

Everyone raised their hands. Even Wen and Man-Man – they didn't want to be the only ones *not* to vote for Mo. That would make them very unpopular with everyone else.

It was a landslide victory for Mo.

THE DARTBOARD

Mo was in trouble again. He had broken the science class globe – a big one that showed every country in the world. Mr Thunder, the science teacher, asked Mo what he was going to do about the broken globe. Mo said he would buy another one with his pocket money. One exactly the same as the one he'd broken.

"All right then," Mr Thunder said, "You may take the broken globe home and find an identical replacement."

That was supposed to have been that. However, when Man-Man wrote down Mo's latest piece of mischief into her little notebook, it was no longer quite so simple...

The little notebook recorded every single one of Mo's mischiefs. At the end of every school day, Man-Man gave the notebook to Ms Qin, so that Ms Qin could see how Mo had behaved in other classes.

Ms Qin had originally planned to keep Mo in after school for damaging school property. But Mr Thunder said he had already dealt with the matter. Ms Qin, however, wasn't sure that Mo *had* learned his lesson. She asked Man-Man and Lily if they would walk home with Mo and talk to his parents about what he had done.

Mo walked ahead of the two girls carrying the broken globe. Man-Man and Lily walked behind him, keeping their distance so Mo wouldn't talk to them.

When the three of them arrived at Mo's house, neither of Mo's parents were there.

"When will your parents get home?" Man-Man asked.

"Very soon," answered Mo.

But that wasn't true. Mo knew that his father had a

dinner appointment and wouldn't be home until later. Mo also knew that his mother had aerobics class after work and she wouldn't be home soon, either. Mo lied because he didn't want Man-Man and Lily to leave. But that wasn't true either. He didn't mind if Man-Man left. Mo didn't want *Lily* to leave. This was the first time Lily had been to Mo's house, and he wanted her to stay a little longer.

So Mo decided to play the charming host. He couldn't care less why the girls had come to his home. He just wanted to be nice to Lily. She was so pretty, after all!

"Can I get you girls anything to drink?" he asked. Mo knew this was the first thing his father always said to guests.

Mo was trying so hard to impress Lily. But he was too shy to look at her, because he thought he might blush. So it was Man-Man who answered him first.

"What have you got?" she said.

"We've got coke, and we've got yoghurt. Or I could make freshly squeezed fruit juice for you," Mo said.

"Freshly squeezed fruit juice for me." Man-Man said, without hesitation.

"I'll just have water, please," said Lily.

Mo had forgotten that Lily was a ballet dancer – she

was very careful about what she ate and drank.

Mo was cross with himself. It took ages to make freshly-squeezed fruit juice. He wouldn't mind making it for Lily. But it was Man-Man who'd asked for it, and Mo wasn't so thrilled about making it for her.

Man-Man didn't even say thank you when Mo gave her the fruit juice he'd taken the trouble to make for her. She didn't even smile at him.

"Exactly when will your parents be home, Mo?" Man-Man asked.

"Very soon! Very soon," he replied.

Lily was quite enjoying herself. As she sipped her water, she looked around the living room of Mo's flat.

She was staring at the dartboard on the wall. Suddenly, she started laughing.

"Lily, what is it?"

Lily didn't answer – she was laughing so much that she had tears in her eyes.

Man-Man rushed over to look at the dartboard. As soon as she saw what Lily had been laughing at, she turned on Mo.

"Mo, you are SO mean," she said.

"What's wrong?" asked Mo, innocently, "I haven't done anything."

Man-Man pointed at the dartboard. She was so furious that she could hardly get her words out. "What's that then?"

Mo suddenly realised what the girls were looking at. Man-Man's name was written in the centre of the dartboard, right in the middle of the bulls-eye.

Mo couldn't even remember writing it there. He and Man-Man had been fighting and quarrelling for so long.

Mo hated seeing anyone cry. And although Man-Man wasn't actually crying now, Mo felt sorry for her.

"Man-Man, I promise, I have never aimed a single dart at you."

Lily examined the dartboard carefully. She said, "Mo's telling the truth, Man-Man. There's not one single dart mark on your name."

Man-Man felt a little bit better but she wasn't going to forgive Mo just yet. She took out her little notebook and wrote down this latest piece of mischief...

By now, the children had been waiting for ages, but there was still no sign of Mo's parents. Lily had had enough of looking round Mo's living room and wanted to leave.

"Wait, wait! They will be back soon," pleaded Mo.

He really didn't want Lily to leave. He got some fruit jellies from the fridge and offered them to Lily.

But Lily knew that fruit jellies were full of sugar. Her ballet teacher had told her many times to cut out sweets, because sweets would make her gain weight.

Man-Man helped herself. She grabbed a big fruit jelly and finished it in one big gulp. She was still hot and angry about the dartboard – the icy cold fruit jelly was perfect to cool her down. She ate more and more jellies – red, green, yellow, purple and pink jellies all went down her tummy.

How greedy! thought Mo. If he'd known Lily wouldn't eat fruit jellies, he wouldn't have taken them out of the fridge. Even he wasn't as greedy as Man-Man when it came to fruit jellies! He limited himself to just two every day.

Man-Man finished all the fruit jellies. She didn't even thank Mo, she just asked him crossly, "why aren't your parents back yet?"

Mo ignored her question. Then he had an idea.

"Would you like to see some magic tricks?" he asked.

Now he had the girls' attention! Man-Man and Lily weren't in quite such a rush to leave anymore. They wanted to see Mo's magic tricks.

THE MASTER OF MAGIC

Mo went into his bedroom to prepare for his magic show. Man-Man and Lily sat on the sofa in the living room waiting.

The two girls waited... and waited... and waited. Mo still hadn't come out of his room. Had he tricked them and vanished? If he had, it wasn't a very good magic trick...

"If you don't come out this minute, we're going!" Man-Man yelled.

"TA DAAAAA!"

Mo made a grand entrance. He was wearing a magician's top hat and a swirling black cape, and he was carrying a wand. He'd put a black false moustache in between his nose and mouth.

"Behold the Master of Magic, the Miraculous, the Marvellous, the Mighty Mo Shen Ma!" Mo threw his cape around his body and made a deep bow to the girls.

Mo waited for his applause, but there was just a bit of giggling.

"What do you think he looks like?" Lily whispered to Man-Man.

"He looks like a big crow," said Man-Man. "A big crow, with a moustache!"

Mo suddenly lost his confidence.

"Do you know any tricks or not?" Man-Man asked impatiently.

"Yes. The magic show starts now." Mo called out the name of his first trick. "The Master of Magic's first trick is called, 'Snowflakes from the palm of my hand'."

Mo took out a paper fan. He held the fan in his right hand and showed them his left hand. "Look closely now, do you see anything in my left hand?"

Lily shook her head. Man-Man just watched.

The fan moved from Mo's right hand to left, and then back to the right hand again. Mo made a fist with his left hand, and started rubbing something in his left fist very hard.

"ABRACADABRA, let there be snow," he shouted.

Then Mo fanned his left fist with the fan in his right hand very hard. He gradually loosened his left fist, and a lot of paper scraps flew out of his palm. There were so many paper scraps it seemed to be snowing in the living room.

"Mo, that is AMAZING!" Lily was impressed.

But Man-Man asked Mo to show her the fan.

"A magician never shows his magic gadgets," he said, "otherwise the magic will not work."

Mo had learned all of his magic tricks from Mr Thunder, the science teacher.

"I'd like to see you do that trick again," said Man-Man.

Mo thought it was because Man-Man liked his trick. He didn't realise that Man-Man wanted to trick him. But Man-Man thought if she saw it again, she would know how he'd done it…

Mo shut himself in his bedroom again to prepare for the trick.

"Mo, hurry up and come out! Otherwise we're going!" Man-Man said impatiently.

TA DAAAAA! Mo made his grand entrance again. He flung the door open and entered, wrapping his cape around him in a grand gesture. The girls giggled again.

When the snowflakes were flying in the room, Mo got a round of applause.

"Fantastic! Brilliant!" Lily clapped so hard, that for a few seconds, Mo was the happiest boy on earth. But it didn't last.

Man-Man snatched the fan from Mo's hand and saw there was a broken thread tied up to the fan.

"I know how this trick works," she said, triumphantly.

Man-Man started explaining. "You spent ages in your room because you were tearing up little bits of paper. The paper scraps were put into a paper pocket, and the paper pocket was tied to the thread, which was tied to the fan. As you were holding the fan, you hid the paper pocket in your palm, so there was no way we could have seen it. After you showed us that your left hand was empty, you placed the fan and the pocket into your left hand and then moved the fan back to the right hand again. But the pocket was still hidden in your left hand. At that point, you broke the thread, and started fanning your left hand. Meanwhile, your left hand was rubbing very hard to tear the paper pocket. When you let go of your left hand, the paper scraps come flying out."

Mo was dumbfounded. Was Man-Man some kind of witch that could see *everything*?

It was VICTORY for Man-Man.

"Has the Master of Magic, the so-called Marvellous, Miraculous Mo Shen Ma, any other tricks to show us?" she asked, rather nastily.

If he was going to show them something else, he had to make sure it was something really good, something that Man-Man couldn't see through...

"I will show you something called 'eggs in glasses'," Mo said, mysteriously.

Now "eggs in glasses" wasn't really a trick. It was a party piece that took great skill. Mo had practised for ages before he did it in front of his friends at his birthday party last year. He decided he would try it again, this time in front of the girls.

 91

Mo began preparing, his cape sweeping around the floor.

Man-Man thought Mo looked ridiculous. "Stop pretending you're a magician Mo. I saw through your trick."

Mo was feeling rather ashamed that Man-Man had caught him out. So he took off his cape and hat, and even snatched off his false moustache.

Mo placed four glasses filled with water on the table. A thin wooden board was used to cover the mouths of the glasses; then four paper circular bands were placed on the wooden board, exactly above the mouths of the glasses. He placed an egg in the centre of each paper band.

"Pay attention now, I am about to start!" Mo rubbed his hands, "As soon as I knock on the wooden board, the eggs will fall into the glass underneath."

Mo held up his hands and started making a pushing gesture.

"What are you doing?" Man-Man asked.

"I am gathering up strength from my entire body."

Man-Man walked closer and stood next to Mo.

92

"Hurry up and knock the board!"

Mo knocked on the board with one hand. The board flew out, so did the eggs, landing in a mess of yolks and whites.

"Ha-ha!

"Ha-ha!"

Man-Man and Lily fell about laughing. "That was spectacular," said Man-Man. "A spectacular MESS!"

Mo felt terrible. How could he make such a fool of himself? How could he make such a mess? He hadn't made that mistake last time he did it. It was all Man-Man's fault. He had to get his own back...

BRAINTEASERS

Mo wanted to try again, but he thought his mother might be cross if he broke any more eggs.

"I don't want to watch it again anyway!" pouted Man-Man. "Now, Mo, when are your parents going to be here?"

Man-Man was determined to wait for Mo's parents to get home. She wanted to tell them about Mo breaking the school globe, and how he had to buy another globe to replace the broken one.

"They won't be long now," Mo fibbed. He had to think of something else to keep the girls entertained.

Then Mo had an idea! He remembered that Dad had given him a book of brainteasers for his birthday last year.

"Let's play brainteasers," he said. "I'll ask the questions, and you two can answer. Whoever answers the fastest and gets the most answers right, wins."

"I don't want to play that," said Lily, "brainteasers make my brain hurt."

"I don't either," said Man-Man. "Brainteasers are boring!"

"Well," said Mo. "Angel is very good at brainteasers, she *always* gets them right. I wonder if Man-Man can beat Angel. Probably not."

"Is Angel *really* clever with brainteasers?" said Man-Man, amazed that Angel could be better than her at anything.

"If you don't believe me, I'll go and get her," said Mo. "Then we can have a brainteaser competition until my parents come home."

Angel's flat was right across the hall from Mo's, so it didn't take long for her to come over. Mo asked Angel and Man-Man to sit opposite each other at the table, while he sat at one end of the table to ask the questions. Lily sat at the other end, as she was going to be the judge.

Mo found his brainteaser book and flipped to a random page. Then he started reading the question.

"Listen carefully now:

I can run, but never walk,

I sometimes babble but never talk,

I have a bed but never sleep,

I have a mouth but never eat.

What am I?"

"A robot!" Man-Man was the first to answer.

"Wrong!"

"It's a river," Angel said.

"Congratulations!" said Mo, in the voice of a TV quizmaster. "*River* is the correct answer!"

Mo flipped to another page and asked the second question, "Listen carefully now – a man is walking on a beach, he looks back but can't see his footprints, why?"

"Because he was invisible!" Man-Man said.

Man-Man had seen a film called The Invisible Man. She knew an invisible man couldn't leave footprints. Man-Man was *positive* she'd got that one right.

"Wrong. There's no such thing as an invisible man!" said Mo. "Except in films. Angel, what's your answer?"

"The man was walking backwards." Angel said.

"Congratulations! "'A man walking backwards' is the correct answer!"

"Yes!" Angel was pleased with herself.

Man-Man was growing suspicious. She looked at Mo and then at Angel, wondering whether the two of them had planned the whole thing to make her look bad. How could Angel get the answers right when she couldn't? And she was the best student in the class!

"Mo, are you asking questions that Angel already knows the answers to?"

"Are you saying we're *cheating*?"

Mo gave the brainteaser book to Lily. "If you think we're cheating, let's ask Lily to pick the questions."

Lily was happy to ask the questions.

"Listen carefully now – what's black and white and read all over?"

Angel waited for Man-Man to answer first. But Man-Man said, "That's a stupid question, how can something be black and white if it is red?"

Lily said, "OK, I'll offer it to the other side. Angel – what is black and white and read all over?"

"A NEWSPAPER!" laughed Angel. It was a trick question.

"Congratulations! 'A newspaper' is the correct answer!"

Man-Man was furious. "That's NOT FAIR," she said, "you shouldn't be asking trick questions!"

Mo laughed so hard his tummy hurt. "OK, no more trick brainteasers. Lily, ask some more questions."

"Listen carefully now – a man fell from an airplane but he wasn't killed. Why?"

"I know!" Man-Man answered confidently, "The man was a rubber-man."

"No," Lily hinted. "The man was a real man, not a rubber-man. Try again."

But Man-Man wasn't going to give in. "Only a rubber-man could fall from so high up and not get hurt."

"I know! I know!" said Angel. "The aeroplane hadn't taken off; so the man wasn't killed when he fell from it."

"Congratulations! 'The aeroplane hadn't taken off' is the correct answer!"

"I'm so stupid! Why didn't I think of that?" Man-Man was so annoyed with herself, she desperately wanted to win.

Seeing that Man-Man was getting so serious, Lily started getting a little worried.

"Let's end this game, shall we?" Lily whispered to Man-Man.

"Why should we?" Man-Man wasn't a good loser.

"There's no way Angel is going to beat me."

"All right then. Listen carefully now – the bell rang, but there wasn't a single pupil in the classroom. Why?"

"Because the bell rang for the end of a PE class, and everyone was in the gym!" Man-Man said.

"Congratulations! Man-Man, 'everyone was in the gym' is the correct answer!"

Lily beamed at Man-Man, and Man-Man suddenly grew more confident.

"Lily, go on!"

"Listen carefully now – Why does a rocket travel so fast?"

"Because its backside is on fire." Angel said quickly.

"Congratulations! 'Its backside is on fire' is the correct answer!"

"Listen carefully now – a building was leaking rainwater everywhere, but no one was getting wet. Why?"

"The building was empty." Angel said.

"Congratulations! 'The building was empty' is the correct answer!"

"Listen carefully now – why did the chicken cross the road?"

"To get to the other side," yelled Angel.

"Congratulations! 'To get to the other side' is the correct answer!

"Listen carefully now—"

"Stop it! Stop it! I'm not playing anymore!" Man-Man screamed. "I'm going home!"

Angel got so many answers right, it was obvious Man-Man was going to lose.

"Man-Man, please don't go! It was only a game." Mo stood by the door. "Anyway, Mum and Dad will be home soon!"

"Get out of my way, Mo!"

Losing to Angel – Man-Man couldn't *believe* it! She was so upset she had forgotten why she'd come home with Mo in the first place. She pushed him aside and rushed out of the door into the landing. She rang the bell for the lift and when it arrived she stepped in, just as Mo's father was stepping out.

"Hello young lady," he said. "Aren't you Ms Man-Man?"

But before Man-Man had time to reply, the lift door had closed.

"Dad, Man-Man was waiting for you for ages. She couldn't wait any longer."

"Well, why did she leave just as I got back?" said Mo's dad.

"You can ask *her*." Mo pointed at Angel. "She made Man-Man upset, so Man-Man left."

But Mo's father knew better than that. He knew his son quite well...

BEST BEHAVED BOY?

There were three kinds of award a class could get at the end of each school term: Best Classroom Display, Best Class Assembly and Best Behaved Class.

Mo's class had won awards for Best Classroom Display and Best Class Assembly, but they had never won the Best Behaved Class... ever.

One day at morning assembly, the head-teacher said she wanted to talk about discipline. She was getting really fed up with children who wouldn't behave properly. She said that Year 4Q – Mo's class – was one of the *worst*-behaved classes in the whole school.

Man-Man, Wen and Lily looked shocked. Ms Qin looked horrified. She was 4Q's class teacher, but she was also one of the best teachers in the entire school. If the head-teacher said her class were badly behaved, then that must mean she was a bad teacher! She decided to have a word with her class monitors at the end of the day. Somehow, she had to get the pupils' behaviour to improve. As the bell rang for the end of school, she asked Man-Man, Lily and Wen if they would stay behind.

"Now, you are three of my best pupils. Pupils I can trust to tell the truth. Why does this class have a reputation for being the worst-behaved in the whole school? Can you tell me?"

Wen was the first to speak.

"Our class's behaviour is bad because we have the Gang of Four in it, and they never behave." Wen said.

The others knew exactly who Wen was talking about: the Gang of Four were Mo, Hippo, Monkey and Penguin.

"Mo is the worst of all," Wen continued. "He doesn't know the first thing about good behaviour."

"Well, that's not quite fair," said Ms Qin. "He was very good at the picnic. We just need to find ways of making him better at school."

"Yes, we must work on Mo," Man-Man agreed. "Let's think of a way to help improve his classroom behaviour."

Wen jumped in again. "Let's make a few simple rules for Mo. For example, if Mo misbehaves in class, he has to clean the classroom for one week."

"I don't think that's a good idea," said Ms Qin. "We have cleaners to clean the classrooms, we wouldn't want them out of a job. We can't use that to punish Mo."

"How about whenever Mo misbehaves, he has to run round the playground ten times?" Man-Man suggested.

"Ten times? He's so full of energy, he'd enjoy that."

"We could ask his parents to come to school every time Mo misbehaves."

"That wouldn't work either. Mo's parents both have jobs, they couldn't just leave their jobs to come to school. Anyway Mo *likes* his parents coming to school." Man-Man knew this more than anyone. "Mo's father thinks it's normal for boys to be naughty. He says it's in their nature. He thinks Mo's antics are funny."

"I have an idea," said Lily. "Remember at the picnic, how much Mo loved being team leader? Why don't we make him some kind of classroom leader, give him a job he loves doing?"

"How would that improve his behaviour?" said Wen. "He'd just be bossy all the time."

But Ms Qin thought Lily had a point. She asked Lily what kind of leadership position they should give Mo.

"How about we make him *Behaviour* Monitor?"

Every class had a Book Monitor, a Playground Monitor, a Games Monitor and a Pencil and Paper Monitor.... but no class had a Behaviour Monitor. Behaviour was something adults usually had to sort out.

Ms Qin was at her wit's end when it came to Mo. She was prepared to try anything. She decided to give Lily's idea a try. She told Man-Man and Lily they could ask Mo if he would accept the position of Behaviour Monitor.

The following day, Man-Man told Mo about their meeting.

"Mo, there was a meeting after school yesterday."

"So? What does that have to do with me?" Mo said indifferently.

"Well, it has everything to do with you," said Man-Man. "You're going to be given a responsible job to do in the class."

"Stop joking. You're just trying to trick me." Mo knew Man-Man wanted to get her own back after losing the brainteaser competition. He wasn't going to fall for it.

Man-Man and Mo fought all the time. If Man-Man suggested something, Mo would always do the opposite just to annoy her. So Man-Man knew what she had to do to make Mo believe her.

"Mo, you'd better accept this offer or else. It was *Lily* who nominated you."

Lily had nominated Mo for a responsible job? Mo grew even more suspicious. Lily never seemed particularly friendly towards him. But he wished she would be! He would do anything for Lily, even if she asked him to jump into a sea of sharks.

So if Lily had really nominated him… he had to do it.

Mo turned around and asked Lily who sat right

behind him, "Did you really nominate me for a responsible classroom job?"

"Yes, Mo," Lily said. "I nominated you to be class Behaviour Monitor."

"What does a Behaviour Monitor do?"

"The Behaviour Monitor is in charge of making sure the class behaves. If our class misbehaves, it's your responsibility to sort it out."

"It wasn't *my* idea," said Man-Man, quickly. "You're the worst-behaved boy in our class, so I think it's stupid to give you the job."

Mo fell for it. "I don't care if you think it's a stupid idea. Lily nominated me, not you. And what's more, I accept the position of Class 4Q Behaviour Monitor. And that's that!"

"Yes!" giggled Man-Man and Lily.

MO SETS AN EXAMPLE

Ms Qin told the class that Mo had been appointed Behaviour Monitor, and that his duties would begin this afternoon.

The first class in the afternoon was science.

As soon as the bell rang, Mo stood at the teacher's desk and said loudly to the class, "Back to your seats! Back to your seats! The class is about to start!"

"What a show-off," Monkey whispered to Hippo. He thinks he's in charge."

"Monkey, stop talking!"

Monkey turned around and spoke to Penguin on purpose, "Did I talk?"

"Nope." Penguin shook his head.

"Monkey and Penguin, I am going to write your names on the blackboard."

Mo wasn't joking, he really wrote down their names on the blackboard.

"I didn't talk!" Penguin protested angrily.

Then Mo saw Wen sniggering. He shouted, "Wen, stop sniggering!"

But there was no way Wen was going to let Mo boss him around.

"I was only sniggering. You can't tell me to stop sniggering."

"Yes I can!" Mo stared at Wen, "I am the Behaviour Monitor!"

"You're a pain in the neck, that's what you are!"

But Mo wrote down Wen's name on the blackboard too.

Wen turned to Man-Man. "Man-Man, are you going to do something about Mo or not?"

Man-Man was just thinking that Mo was going a bit too far. But before she had the chance to say anything, Mo had written her name on the blackboard.

"I haven't said anything yet. Why did you write down my name?"

"You were *listening* to Wen."

Chaos broke out in the class.

"Be quiet! Be quiet!" Mo ordered, feeling self-important, "If you don't be quiet this moment, I will write all of your names on the blackboard."

When Mr Thunder walked in, he couldn't understand why Mo was standing by his desk.

"What are you doing there?" Mr Thunder asked.

"I am now the class Behaviour Monitor." Mo replied, proudly. "I am in charge of disciplining the whole class."

Mr Thunder wanted to laugh, but he couldn't let the children see that. That scamp, Mo. How could someone that naughty and mischievous be Behaviour Monitor? He patted Mo on the shoulder. "Well, Mo. Everyone is behaving themselves now. You can go back to your seat."

Mo reluctantly returned to his seat. He wanted to stand in front of the class for the whole lesson. He liked his new job.

Mr Thunder was about to begin the lesson. He saw several names written crookedly on the blackboard and was just about to rub them out when he heard Mo call out; "Don't rub out the names, Mr Thunder! Those are the children who misbehaved."

Man-Man was so mad at Mo that she stepped hard on his foot.

"Ouuuuch!!!"

"All right, I won't rub them out. What were you yelling for?" Mr Thunder asked.

"Man-Man stepped on my foot on purpose!"

Mr Thunder told Man-Man to stop and that she should know better.

Man-Man began to regret the fact that she had agreed to let Mo be Behaviour Monitor.

After the second lesson in the afternoon was over, Mo had written more than twenty children's names on the blackboard.

The next lesson was 'self-study'.

This was when children could do their homework while Ms Qin prepared for lessons or corrected children's project work. Today however, as soon as Ms Qin entered the classroom, she saw the long list of names on the blackboard.

"What is this?" she asked

"Those are the children who misbehaved this afternoon," Mo called out.

"What did Wen do?" Ms Qin asked.

"Wen laughed at me and called me a pain in the neck."

Everyone laughed. Ms Qin frowned.

"And Man-Man? What did she do wrong?" Ms Qin said.

"Man-Man stepped on my foot on purpose," replied Mo.

 113

The class broke into laughter again.

The class finally calmed down after a few minutes. Ms Qin began to mark some coursework, and everyone else started to do their homework.

Mo was the only one who wasn't doing anything. He was looking around the classroom, and listening for any sound that hinted of misbehaviour.

Aha – what was that he could hear?! He could hear food being chewed. It must be Penguin.

"Stop eating in the classroom, Penguin!"

Penguin was chewing gum.

"I am not eating anything." Penguin hid the gum underneath his tongue and opened his mouth to show Mo.

As soon as Penguin opened up his mouth, Mo could smell the scent of mint. He knew Penguin must have hidden the gum underneath his tongue.

Ms Qin walked over, and Penguin opened up his mouth to show Ms Qin.

"The gum is underneath his tongue." Mo said.

Ms Qin asked Penguin to twist his tongue aside, and there it was: the gum that was hidden underneath!

Mo had done a good job. He was going to try even harder.

Mo's sense of smell was extraordinary. Next he could smell stinky feet. Someone must have taken off their shoes. And that someone had to be Hippo. No one's feet were as stinky as Hippo's.

Mo crawled underneath his desk to see if Hippo had taken off his shoes.

"Mo, what do you think you are doing?" Ms Qin asked.

"Ms Qin, someone is polluting the air that we breathe." Mo pointed at Hippo. "Hippo has taken his shoes off!"

"Phewy, Pongy, what a stink!"

Once Mo had said it, everyone in the classroom could smell stinky feet. All the children picked up their exercise books and tried to fan away the horrible smell.

Ms Qin told Hippo to put his shoes back on his feet.

Another job well done! Mo decided to work even harder.

Ms Qin walked round the classroom. She looked at Mo's exercise book and saw that he hadn't begun his homework. "Mo," she said quietly, "it's good that you're worrying about your fellow pupils' behaviour, but I would like *you* to behave and get on with your homework!"

TROUBLEMAKER

Ever since Mo had been Behaviour Monitor, the overall behaviour of the class had improved. As Mo wrote down names of children breaking classroom rules on to the blackboard, the troublemakers were all forced to behave: Monkey, normally a chatter-box, stopped talking in class; Penguin, who always secretly ate in classroom, had to wait till playtime; Hippo, who liked to take his shoes off in class, had to keep them on. At the next school assembly, the head-teacher announced that Mo's class had improved so much, they had won the Best Behaved Class award.

Mo thought it only natural that *he* should be the one to receive the award from the head-teacher, since he was the Behaviour Monitor. So, as soon as their class was called, Mo got ready to go up to the platform.

"Mo, what do you think you are doing?" Ms Qin said sternly.

"I … I am going to get the award."

"Who asked you to go up there? Sit down this minute."

Mo sat down, looking crestfallen. Ms Qin asked Man-Man to go and get the award.

Mo wasn't happy, but he soon dutifully went back to being Behaviour Monitor. In the afternoon, the blackboard was again filled with names – children who Mo judged to have broken classroom rules. Over half of the children in the class had their names written on the blackboard!

Everyone was fed up with Mo being Behaviour Monitor. Some complained to Ms Qin, telling her how unfair Mo was.

"Ms Qin, I accidentally sneezed in class, and just because of that, Mo wrote my name on the blackboard!"

"Ms Qin, my hair came loose in PE class, and just

because I tied back my hair, Mo wrote my name on the blackboard!"

"Ms Qin, I couldn't answer a question in Maths. Even the Maths teacher said I shouldn't worry, but Mo still wrote down my name on the blackboard!"

It wasn't only the children who complained to Ms Qin about Mo. Other teachers did too.

"Ms Qin, Mo was causing a lot of trouble in Music," The music teacher said.

It was during a singing lesson. The music teacher asked the children to place their hands over their tummies and feel whether their tummies were expanding and contracting while they were singing. But Mo didn't do as he had been asked. He was too busy watching everybody else's tummy, to see if they were expanding and contracting. When he saw a child whose tummy was not expanding and contracting, he made a big fuss about it.

The Music teacher was forced to stop the lesson and ask, "Mo, what is all the fuss about?"

"Wen's tummy isn't expanding and contracting."

"Mo, you shouldn't be worrying about other people's tummies. You should be worrying about your own!"

"But I'm the Behaviour Monitor!"

The music teacher didn't know whether to laugh or cry.

Not only did Mo cause trouble in music class, he also created havoc in PE class.

Half way through the PE class, the teacher asked the girls to do mat exercises and the boys to run laps. The playground wasn't big enough for running laps, so the children were allowed to use the school drive.

It usually took ten minutes for the boys to finish their laps. But on this particular day, the boys were late getting back to class.

The PE teacher was worried. Had something happened?

He rushed outside to find the boys. They were all standing in the middle of the road. Now the teacher was really worried. Had there been an accident?

He reached the group of boys.

"If you've finished your laps you should be back in the PE class. What are you all doing in the middle of the road?"

Everyone talked at once and the teacher couldn't hear properly.

"One at a time!"

"Mo was being bossy, he kept telling us to go faster and faster and do more laps. We got fed up with him and he tried to start a fight."

The PE teacher couldn't understand why Mo was acting so oddly. He was always up to mischief, but he wasn't the sort of boy to start a fight.

"I am the Behaviour Monitor," Mo said. "But they wouldn't do what I asked."

"Ms Qin," said the teachers. "You'll have to stop Mo being Behaviour Monitor. He's getting too big for his boots."

Ms Qin knew it. In fact, she was regretting agreeing to Mo being Behaviour Monitor. Lily's idea had been a good one, but it hadn't really worked. Ms Qin called Mo into her office.

"Mo, how do you think you did being Behaviour Monitor?"

"I did a good job! Our class has never won the Best Behaviour award before, so I must have done a good job."

"But *everyone* in the class worked hard to get that award! Not just you, Mo."

"But I'm the Behaviour Monitor. So I must have worked harder than everybody else."

"Mo, do you know *why* you were chosen to be Behaviour Monitor?"

"Because Lily nominated me."

Ms Qin shook her head.

"But she did! Man-Man told me so."

But that wasn't quite was Ms Qin meant. Ms Qin wanted to know if Mo knew *why* he'd been chosen for the job.

"Why? So that I could make sure the other children behaved," Mo said. "I showed them who was boss. I wrote their names down if they had done things wrong."

Ms Qin knew that she had to tell Mo the truth.

"Mo," she said, gently. "You were given the job of Behaviour Monitor, so that you could start behaving *yourself*. It was to make *your* behaviour better... as well as everyone else's," she quickly added.

"Oh," whispered Mo.

Then Ms Qin said he had to stop being Behaviour Monitor. Mo looked at the floor, then he looked at Ms Qin and said in his best teacher's-pet voice, "Ms Qin, will you come home and meet my parents?"

"Whatever for, Mo?"

"To prove that I *was* the Behaviour Monitor."

"Why do you need to prove that?" asked Ms Qin.

"My dad wouldn't believe me. And now you've removed me from my post, he won't ever believe me. So, I want you to tell him. He'll believe you," Mo explained.

How could Ms Qin refuse? Mo was always up to mischief, but he really wanted his parents to be proud of him. Ms Qin agreed to go to Mo's flat after school.

When Ms Qin met Mo's father, she told him that what Mo had said was true, that he really *had* been class Behaviour Monitor – at least for a little while!

"Mo, that's fantastic news. You finally did something to make me proud!" Mo's father gave Mo a big hug. Ms Qin felt a tear coming to her eye.

"Mr Mo," she said, kindly. There is something else I need to tell you. Mo isn't Behaviour Monitor anymore."

"What do you mean?"

Mo's father stopped hugging his son.

"Mr Ma," Ms Qin explained, "Mo did such a good job as Behaviour Monitor that our class won the Best Behaved Class award. So Mo didn't need to do the job anymore."

"How long did he do the job for?" Mo's father asked.

"One week."

"Just one week, Mo?"

"Yes, Dad, I'm a speedy worker!

Mo's father ruffled his son's hair. "One whole week of good behaviour! I never would have believed it!"

READER'S NOTE

MO'S WORLD

Mo Shen Ma lives in a big city in China. Modern Chinese cities are very much like ours, so his life is not so different from your own: he goes to school, watches television and gets up to mischief – just like children all over the world!

There are *some* differences, though. Chinese writing is completely unlike our own. There is no alphabet, and words are not made up of letters – instead, each word is represented by a little drawing called a *character*. For us, learning to read is easy. There are only twenty-six letters that make up all our words! But in Chinese, every word has its own character. Even Simplified Chinese writing uses a core of 6,800 different characters. Each character has to be learned by heart, which means that it takes many years for a Chinese school student to learn to read fluently

NAMES

Chinese personal names carry various meanings and the names in this book have definitely been chosen for a reason! Take Mo Shen, the hero of our tale. His name is made up of the word *Mo*, which means "good ideas" and *Shen*, which means "deep" or "profound". So you can see how much his name suits him, because Mo Shen is always coming up with great ideas!

Then there's Mo's arch-rival, Man-Man. Her name means "really slow". This is because in China there is a tradition of giving children names that are the exact opposite of their real character. The last thing Man-Man could be accused of being is slow!

Mo's other rival is Wen Tao Ting. *Wen* means "to do with books", and *Tao* means "big and strong as a wave". So Wen Tao Ting is very strong when it comes to books! This fits well with his nickname, "Little Encyclopaedia".

STORY BACKGROUND

You will have noticed that Mo's school is slightly different to ours. It seems like the pupils are constantly competing against one another for prizes, even when it comes to cooking! Discipline is also more rigid than we are used to.

Chinese schools, especially in the large cities, are highly competitive. This is partly due to the sheer size of the country, which means that for the sake of efficiency, every school teaches the same subjects using the same materials. And it's not hard to see why a universal system is necessary – there are over eight *million* schools in China! Pupils in Chinese primary schools are expected to be strong in all subject areas, rather than specialising – this results in inevitable comparisons between different pupils in a class, and even between different schools.

Someone like Mo, who goes to an urban school, can expect the competition to continue as he moves through the school system. University places are limited and are hotly contested between high-school pupils, meaning that Mo will keep having to out-do Man-Man and Wen as he gets older!